BIG SURPRISE in the BUG TANK

A Puffin Easy-to-Read

by Ruth Horowitz
pictures by Joan Holub

PUFFIN BOOKS

This one's for Sam. At last.
—R. H.

For Barton Hill and Darlene Hale,
and lunches in Rockport
—J. H.

PUFFIN BOOKS
Published by the Penguin Group
Penguin Young Readers Group, 345 Hudson Street, New York, New York 10014, U.S.A.
Penguin Group (Canada), 90 Eglinton Avenue East, Suite 700, Toronto, Ontario, Canada M4P 2Y3
(a division of Pearson Penguin Canada Inc.)
Penguin Books Ltd, 80 Strand, London WC2R 0RL, England
Penguin Ireland, 25 St Stephen's Green, Dublin 2, Ireland
(a division of Penguin Books Ltd)
Penguin Group (Australia), 250 Camberwell Road, Camberwell, Victoria 3124, Australia
(a division of Pearson Australia Group Pty Ltd)
Penguin Books India Pvt Ltd, 11 Community Centre, Panchsheel Park, New Delhi - 110 017, India
Penguin Group (NZ), Cnr Airborne and Rosedale Roads, Albany, Auckland 1310, New Zealand
(a division of Pearson New Zealand Ltd)
Penguin Books (South Africa) (Pty) Ltd, 24 Sturdee Avenue, Rosebank, Johannesburg 2196, South Africa

Registered Offices: Penguin Books Ltd, 80 Strand, London WC2R 0RL, England

First published in the United States of America by Dial Books for Young Readers,
a division of Penguin Young Readers Group, 2005
Published by Puffin Books, a division of Penguin Young Readers Group, 2006

1 3 5 7 9 10 8 6 4 2

THE LIBRARY OF CONGRESS HAS CATALOGED THE DIAL BOOKS EDITION AS FOLLOWS:
Horowitz, Ruth.
Big surprise in the bug tank / by Ruth Horowitz ; pictures by Joan Holub.
p. cm.
Summary: Two brothers get two giant hissing cockroaches as pets and
then must figure out a way to deal with the resulting population explosion.
ISBN: 0-8037-2874-3 (hc)
[1. Brothers—Fiction. 2. Cockroaches—Fiction. 3. Pets—Fiction. 4. Humorous stories.]
I. Holub, Joan, ill. II. Title. PZ7.H7877Bi 2005 [Fic]—dc22 2003019504

Special Markets ISBN 0-14-240726-7
Puffin® and Easy-to-Read® are registered trademarks of Penguin Group (USA) Inc.

Manufactured in China

Reading Level 2.4

The art was created using watercolor, gouache, and acrylic paints on Arches watercolor paper.

Contents

BUG BUDDIES

Our mom has the coolest job.

She works in a lab where they study

all sorts of weird bugs.

Of all her bugs, the ones we like best

are the giant hissing cockroaches.

One day my brother, Leo, asked

if we could take some home.

"Pretty please with fruit flies on top?"

Leo begged.

"Having pets takes work," Mom warned.

"We will be great bug-sitters," I said.

"Cross our hearts and hope to fly."

So Mom let us each choose a roach.

Leo liked the bumps on his bug's head.

"I will call you Lumpy," he said.

My bug hissed nice and loud.

"Your name is Buzz," I told it.

"If these two bugs are together,

you may have a problem," said Mom.

"Don't worry," said Leo.

"We will make sure they get along."

We gave our bugs dog food to eat

and a toilet paper tube to sleep in.

Sometimes Lumpy slept in the food

and Buzz bit the tube.

One day we saw little white things

all over Buzz's bottom.

"There's rice in the bug tank!" I said.

"That is not rice," said Mom.

"Lumpy and Buzz have six babies."

"I am a bug daddy!" Leo cheered.

After six months, the babies had grown as

big as Buzz and Lumpy.

Baby Curly had

a crooked feeler.

Little Twirly

walked in circles.

Pokey was slow and Dash was fast.

Flash liked to hang

upside down and show off

its pale belly.

Crash liked to bump into walls.

We were as happy as ants on a pizza.

"But soon the babies will have babies,
and then the babies' babies
will have babies," Mom told us.
"This tank will be swarming with bugs!"

"What should we do?" I asked.

"You boys are sharp as wasp stings,"
Mom said. "I bet you can work it out."

ROACHES FOR SALE

"Mom's right," said Leo.

"I can work this out.

I bet you a million bucks."

"If you're wrong," I told him,

"we will be up to our armpits in bugs!"

The next day Leo put a table outside.

I put the roach tank on the table.

Then we made a big sign that said:

ROACHES: ONE DOLLAR.

A lady came toward the table.

"Look at your smile,"

Leo said to the lady.

"That is the smile of a roach lover."

The lady was not just smiling.

She was laughing so hard, she shook.

"Roaches, one dollar!" she shouted.

She was still giggling as she left.

"Strike one," I told Leo.

"Shh. Here comes a man," he said.

This man was not laughing.

"Roaches, one dollar!" he yelled.

"Roaches are nasty and creepy!"

"Strike two," I told Leo.

But he said, "Do not worry, Sam.

"Look at this girl coming now.

If this kid does not buy a roach,

I will give you a million bucks."

17

"Roaches, one dollar!" the girl hollered.

"Can I have one? Can I? Can I?"

"Silly Sally," said the kid's mom.

"You already have a mouse and a horse.

You do not need a roach."

"I do so need one!" Sally screamed.

"Please stop that," Sally's mom begged,

"and I will rent you a Space Slime video."

"Why can't I have both?" Sally asked

as her mom pulled her away.

"Strike three," I told Leo.

"Now where's my million bucks?"

ROACH SURPRISES

"I know what to do," I told Leo.

"People love surprises.

If our roaches are surprises,

people will love them too.

I bet you fifty Big Burp sodas."

We found some boxes in the attic

and pasted fancy paper on them.

Inside each box, we put dog food,

a toilet paper tube, and three roaches.

We taped a note on top that said:

A SURPRISE FOR YOU!

Then we rode to Uncle Joe's house.

"Do you like surprises?" we asked him.

Uncle Joe grinned. "Do I ever!"

"Surprise!" we yelled, lifting the lid.

But Uncle Joe's grin was gone.

"What in the world?" he asked.

"They are giant roaches," I told him.

"They make great pets," Leo added.

But Uncle Joe said, "No thanks, boys.

"I already have a horse."

"Strike one," said Leo.

Next, we went to see Aunt Flo.

"Do you like surprises?" we asked her.

"I think so," she said.

"Surprise!" we yelled.

Aunt Flo just stared into the box.

"Aunt Flo, meet Flash," I said.

"Flash wants to be your friend."

"I'll stick to my fish," said Aunt Flo.

"Strike two," said Leo.

Leo and I went back to Mom.

"When I have a problem," she told us,

"I take it to the library."

"You are one smart mom," I said.

"As bright as a firefly," Leo added.

Our librarian is Mr. Lee.

He collects buttons, tops, and teapots.

We showed him our roaches.

"My word," he said. "You are lucky

to have such neat bugs!"

"You are lucky too," I told him.

"These roach babies are for you!"

"I'm sorry," said Mr. Lee.

"I cannot care for these bugs.

It scares me to touch them."

"Looks like strike three," said Leo.

"Are you sure?" I asked Mr. Lee.
"If we do not find them good homes,
we will be up to our eyeballs in bugs."
Leo and I looked as sad as we could.

"Well, maybe I can help," said Mr. Lee.

"Kids love odd pets.

Let's have an odd pet contest

here in the library.

Your roaches can be the prizes."

"Great idea," I told Mr. Lee.

"You saved our eyeballs," added Leo.

ROACH PRIZES

On the day of the odd pet contest,

one boy brought a tiny toy boat.

A girl brought a potato plant.

Another boy had a pet we could not see.

"I have a huge lion," he said.

"If you could see him,

he'd roar you right out of your seats.

But my lion is very shy."

A girl with lots of braids

had a rope with a rock on one end.

"My pet is called Rocky," she said.

A boy with a buzz cut bragged,

"I can wear my pet around my neck,

and he only eats once a month."

The boy pulled out a snake.

"My pet is a monkey,"

said a girl in a baseball cap.

She held her baby brother.

He had a tail taped to his diaper.

At last it was our turn.

"Our pets are so cool,

grown-ups will not touch them,"

said Leo. "They hiss like snakes

and can hang upside down.

They eat dog food,

and sometimes toilet paper tubes.

Today may be your lucky day.

If you have what it takes,

we may let you take home a bug."

Leo and I reached into the box.

When we pulled out our hands,

roaches were hanging all over them.

The crowd went wild.

Kids cheered, "Awesome!"

and some yelled, "Gross!"

The girl in the cap shouted,

"I will trade you my monkey-baby

for two of those giant roaches!"

"Put out your hand," said Leo.

The girl put out her hand

but then she jumped back.

"I'll keep my monkey," she howled.

The girl with the potato plant

dropped her roach.

It fell on the boy with the shy lion.

The boy calmly handed it to me.

When the pet rock girl held her bug,

it went to sleep in her hand.

"You are even sweeter than a rock,"

the girl said very softly.

At the end of the morning,

the boy with the shy lion, the pet rock girl,

and all the other calm, brave kids

got to keep bug prizes.

"Thanks a million, Mr. Lee," I said.

"You are as clever as a carpenter ant!"

added Leo.

THE BUGS COME BACK

"The library did solve our problem,"
I told Mom when we got home.
We were giving each other high fives
when the phone rang.

"Our house is not a bug house!"
a lady shouted.
"You must take these icky bugs back!"

Then the doorbell buzzed.

A man wearing big gloves held a box.

"You can have this back," he said.

"My son did not mean to win it."

One by one, all our roaches came back.

"Strike three," I sighed.

But Mom said, "Not so fast.

You smart boys *can* solve this problem.

And the library *does* have the answer.

I bet you ten sinks of dirty dishes."

Mom put two roaches in a box

and we all went back to the library.

"Sam! Leo! Who do we have here?"

Mr. Lee said as we came in.

"I think this is Lumpy," said Leo.

"But I am not sure.

Lumpy has bumps on his head,

but so do some of the babies."

"This one does not have bumps," I said.

"Why do you think only some roaches

have bumps?" Mom asked.

"To look extra cool?" Leo guessed.

Mr. Lee took out a big bug book

with a picture of two giant roaches.

One had bumps and the other did not.

"Jumping June bugs!" Leo shouted,
pointing to the words by the picture.
"*A male has horns behind its head,
but a female does not,*" I read.

"I'll be an earwig's uncle," said Leo.

"You knew all along!" I told Mom.

"And I knew *you* could figure it out,"
she said.

Leo and I still have roaches.

But we are not up to our ears in bugs.

All our roaches are males with horns.